Great Figures in History

Gandhi

Mohandas Karamchand Gandhi

Y. kids

www.myykids.com

Great Figures in History

Gandhi

Copyright © 2007 YoungJin Singapore Pte. Ltd.
World rights reserved. No part of this publication may be stored in a retrieval system, transmitted, or reproduced in any way, including but not limited to photocopy, photograph, magnetic, or other record, without the prior agreement and written permission of the publisher.

ISBN: 978-981-054945-9
Printed and bound in the Republic of Korea.

How to contact us
E-mail: feedback@myykids.com

Credits
Adaptation & Art: SAM (Special Academic Manga)
Production Manager: Suzie Lee
Editorial Services: Publication Services, Inc.
Developmental Editor: Rachel Lake, Publication Services, Inc.
Editorial Manager: Lorie Donovan, Publication Services, Inc.
Book Designer: SAM (Special Academic Manga)
Cover Designer: Litmus
Production Control: Jay Won, Misook Kim

CONTENTS

A MESSAGE TO READERS

Welcome to the **Great Figures in History** series by **Y. kids**. These biographies of some of the world's most influential people will take you on an exciting journey through history. These are the stories of great scientists, leaders, artists, and inventors who have shaped the world we live in today.

How did these people make a difference in their world? You will see from their stories that things did not always come easily for them. Just like many of us, they often had problems in school or at home. Some of them had to overcome poverty and hardship. Still others faced discrimination because of their religion, gender, or the color of their skin. But all of these **Great Figures in History** worked tirelessly and succeeded despite many challenges.

Sing, an adventurer from Planet Mud, will be your guide through the lives of these famous historical figures. The people of Sing's planet are in great danger, facing a strange disease that drains their mental powers. To save the people of Planet Mud, Sing must travel through space and time and try to capture the mental powers of several **Great Figures in History**. Will Sing be successful in his journey? You will have to read to find out!

If you enjoy this story, visit our website, **www.myykids.com**, to see other books in the Great Figures in History series. You can also visit the website to let us know what you liked or didn't like about the book, or to leave suggestions for other stories you would like to see.

A NOTE TO PARENTS AND TEACHERS

Y. kids welcomes you to Educational Manga Comics. We certainly hope that your child or student will enjoy reading our books. The Educational Manga Comics present material in "manga" form, a comic story style developed in Japan that is enjoying enormous popularity with young people today. These books deliver substantial educational content in a fun and easy-to-follow visual format.

At the end of each book, you will find bonus features—including a historical timeline, a summary of the individual's enduring cultural significance, and a list of suggested Web and print resources for related information—to enhance your reader's learning experience. Our website, **www.myykids.com**, offers supplemental activities, resources, and study material to help you incorporate **Y. kids** books into your child's reading at home or into a classroom curriculum.

Our entire selection of Educational Manga Comics, covering math, science, history, biographies, and literature, is available on our website. The website also has a feedback option, and we welcome your input.

WHO'S WHO?

Young Gandhi

MOHANDAS GANDHI

A leader of India's independence movement and a founding father of India. He staged a nonviolent civil disobedience movement while India was under British colonial rule. He helped India eventually gain its independence.

PUTLIBAI GANDHI

Gandhi's mother. She was a devoted Hindu and taught Gandhi to keep the Hindu teachings.

KASTRUBA

Gandhi's wife. She married him at the age of 13. She stood by his side throughout his work in the independence movements.

HERBERT ASQUITH

The British Prime Minister. He persuaded Gandhi to convince Indian people to participate in World War I. But he did not free India. Gandhi lost his confidence in the British government after this deceitful action.

LORD IRWIN

The British governor general to India. He tried to suppress the independence movement, but could not defeat Gandhi's persistence in the end.

EXECUTIVES OF THE INDIAN NATIONAL CONGRESS

India's national leaders who fought for independence with Gandhi. The Indian National Congress was organized in 1885. Pandit Jawaharlal Nehru, the first prime minister of India, was one of the members.

SING'S JOURNEY

The residents of Planet Mud in the Andromeda Galaxy have been suffering from a strange illness.

The Planet Mud Disease Control Committee has reported that this plague was caused by a so-called Confusion Virus that drains mental energy from people. Once affected by the virus, people suffer strange symptoms such as tiredness and frustration.

The Planet Mud Disease Control Committee has suggested a solution to this plague. They hope to clone aspects of the mental energy from some of the greatest souls of Planet Earth. When the Cam-cam records the lives of the great souls, it can collect copies of their unique and special mental energy. This mental energy is then refined into crystallized mental energy to be injected into the suffering residents of Planet Mud.

It is Sing's job to collect these crystallized fairies of each great soul's mental energy.

Sing An explorer from Planet Mud. He was dispatched by the Planet Mud Disease Control Committee to collect mental energies from the great souls of Planet Earth.

Alpha Plus Sing's assistant robot who keeps him out of trouble. His vast store of information can solve many questions during their adventures.

Cam-cam An invention from Planet Mud. When it records the lives of the great people, their mental energy is copied and refined.

Courage Fairy This fairy embodies courage, and makes people able to face any difficulties. It gives them the strength to stand up for justice and do what is right.

Porbandar, a territory in West Bengal, India

MOHANDAS, COME ON OUT!

WE BROUGHT YOU SOMETHING!

WE FOUND A DEAD SNAKE LYING ON THE GROUND.

COME HERE, TAKE A LOOK!

HAHAHA

HEY, GO AWAY. I'M SCARED OF SNAKES.

SILLY, IT'S ALREADY DEAD!

9

12

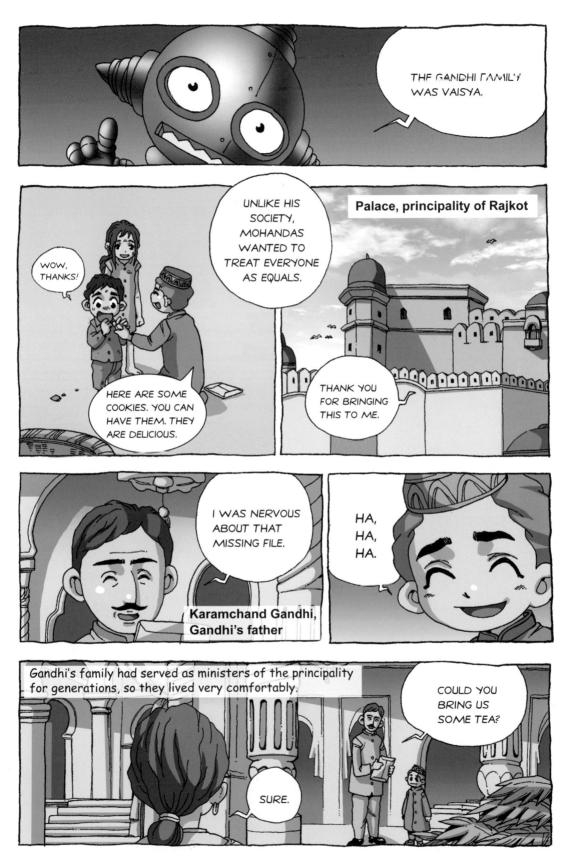

THE GANDHI FAMILY WAS VAISYA.

UNLIKE HIS SOCIETY, MOHANDAS WANTED TO TREAT EVERYONE AS EQUALS.

Palace, principality of Rajkot

WOW, THANKS!

HERE ARE SOME COOKIES. YOU CAN HAVE THEM. THEY ARE DELICIOUS.

THANK YOU FOR BRINGING THIS TO ME.

I WAS NERVOUS ABOUT THAT MISSING FILE.

Karamchand Gandhi, Gandhi's father

HA, HA, HA.

Gandhi's family had served as ministers of the principality for generations, so they lived very comfortably.

COULD YOU BRING US SOME TEA?

SURE.

India had been under British rule since 1858, 11 years before Gandhi was born. The British army in India took all the country's resources and treated the Indian people with merciless violence.

At one point, Indian people joined together to fight against the British, but they couldn't beat the well-trained army of Britain. This event made the Indian people feel even more helpless.

I, I'M SORRY, SIR...

DO YOU THINK YOU CAN LEAVE STAINS ON THE BRITISH ARMY'S SHOES AND BE FORGIVEN SO EASILY?

UGH!

SNATCH

24

Gandhi's mother was a very devoted Hindu. Not only did she go to the temple every day, but she also fasted whenever she prayed for something very important.

....

MOM...

I CAN'T GAIN ANYTHING BY BLAMING THE BRITISH.

IT'S BETTER TO PRAY FOR PEACE IN INDIA.

Faith was an important part of Gandhi's life, too. He was later called "The Saint of India," and his faith guided him to the right path.

WHY DON'T I PRAY UNTIL DAWN TOMORROW?

HINDUISM IS THE NATIONAL RELIGION OF INDIA AND 80% OF THE PEOPLE ARE PRACTICING HINDUS.

PLEASE, GOD. MAY INDIA BE AT PEACE... ZZZ...

I MUST STAY AWAKE, BECAUSE THIS PRAYER IS IMPORTANT.

EPISODE 2
JOURNEY TO ENGLAND

Mohandas grew up well under his mother's teachings.

Mohandas entered middle school in 1881 at the age of 12. At that time, middle school in India lasted six years and included high school courses as well.

Mohandas got married at the age of 13, which was normal at that time in India. He married Kastruba, a girl of the same age.

However, Mohandas's happy family suffered sorrow in 1885, three years after his wedding.

Mohandas's father suddenly passed away from a disease.

Karamchand Gandhi, Minister of Rajkot, May he rest in peace

At his father's funeral, Mohandas decided that he would become a worthy person who worked for the country like his father had.

At age 18, Mohandas entered Samaldas college at Bhavnagar in 1887.

SAMALDAS

YOUNG MAN! IS THAT YOU, MOHANDAS?

?

NO, NO, NO! YOU'RE NOT GOING ANYWHERE!

WHY? WHY CAN'T I GO?

As a devoted Hindu, Gandhi's mother would not eat meat or drink alcohol.

IF YOU GO TO BRITAIN, YOU WILL END UP CONSUMING ALCOHOL AND MEAT! I CAN'T LET YOU GO TO A PLACE LIKE THAT.

Gandhi begged for approval from his mother, who refused. He tried to persuade her over and over again.

DON'T WORRY ABOUT IT, MOM. I SWEAR I WON'T EAT MEAT OR DRINK ALCOHOL. I WILL KEEP THE HINDU DOCTRINES.

On September 4, 1888, Mohandas boarded a ship for England. He was 19 years old.

After two weeks at sea, the ship arrived at London Harbor.

London, capital of the United Kingdom

WOW, WHAT A HUGE CITY!

Great Britain is an island country in western Europe. In the nineteenth century, it was one of the most advanced countries in Europe. With its strong military, it colonized many places around the globe. At its peak, the British Empire ruled a quarter of the world.

British Isles

Union Jack

I'VE FINALLY ARRIVED.

HERE I COME, BRITAIN! MOHANDAS KARAMCHAND GANDHI IS HERE!

···?

I'LL SEE FOR MYSELF IF YOU ARE GOOD ENOUGH TO RULE MY HOME COUNTRY!

WOW, HE SOUNDS AMBITIOUS. NOW HE'S GOING TO MAKE SOMETHING HAPPEN, RIGHT?

IT'S ONLY GOING TO BECOME MORE INTERESTING FROM HERE···

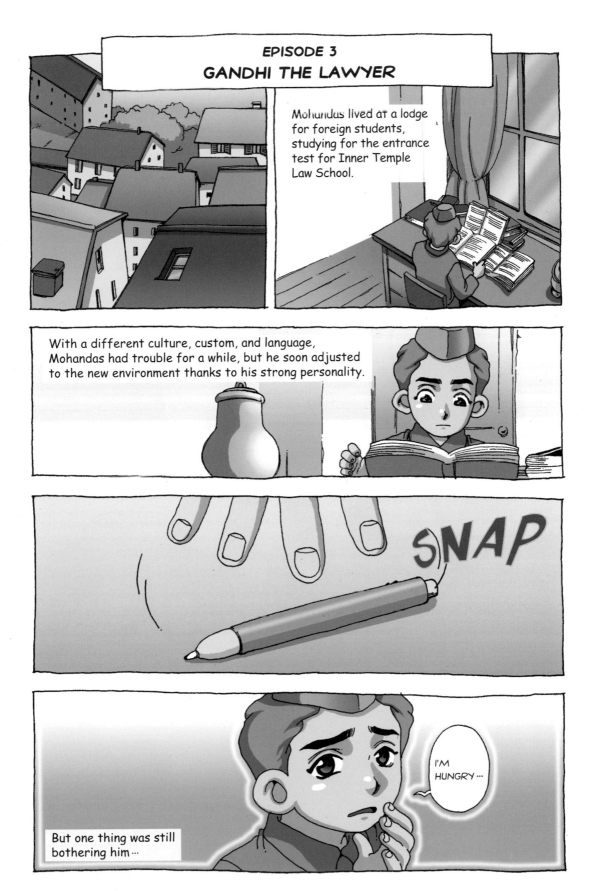

EPISODE 3
GANDHI THE LAWYER

Mohandas lived at a lodge for foreign students, studying for the entrance test for Inner Temple Law School.

With a different culture, custom, and language, Mohandas had trouble for a while, but he soon adjusted to the new environment thanks to his strong personality.

SNAP

I'M HUNGRY...

But one thing was still bothering him...

36

I'VE HAD ENOUGH. ENJOY YOURSELVES.

HE'S NOT EATING AGAIN!

THAT'S GOING TO CAUSE HIM SERIOUS TROUBLE SOMEDAY.

His life in London was a constant struggle with hunger.

He ate steamed vegetables and fruit, but he always felt as if they were not enough.

Whenever this happened, he told himself···

THIS IS JUST A SMALL TRIAL. I'LL GO BACK TO INDIA PROUDLY AFTER I BECOME A LAWYER.

I MUST STUDY HARDER, I CAN DO IT!

HUH!

With his friends, Gandhi went to a social club for the first time.

The fancy parties and beautiful young women in the club were exciting to young Gandhi.

YOU DANCE PRETTY WELL.

!

Dancing was so much fun that Gandhi visited the social club more often.

Little by little, Gandhi couldn't help but neglect his studies.

OH!

Before long, Gandhi took the entrance exam for Inner Temple Law School.

One month later, the admission results were announced.

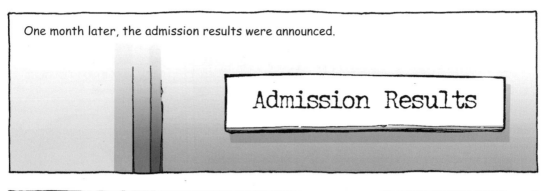

Admission Results

I GOT IN!

ALRIGHT!

I...I'M NOT ON THE LIST.

I FAILED BECAUSE I WAS SPENDING ALL MY TIME DOING SOMETHING OTHER THAN STUDYING.

MOTHER WOULD BE SO DISAPPOINTED IN ME.

I DIDN'T COME HERE TO BE A FAKE ENGLISHMAN. I AM AN INDIAN. I SHOULD LIVE LIKE ONE.

Gandhi threw away his vanity and silly lifestyle with his suit, and started studying hard with a new spirit.

One year later, Gandhi finally succeeded in entering Inner Temple.

Two years later, Gandhi took the bar exam. Law students must pass the bar exam before they can become lawyers.

Bar Exam

MAIL FOR YOU, MR. GANDHI.

June 1891

Bar Exam Results

SNIFFLE

I PASSED!

43

Gandhi finally passed the bar exam after three years in Britain. He was 22 years old.

Lawyer's Certificate

AT LAST, I'M GOING BACK TO INDIA. AND I HAVEN'T BROKEN ANY HINDU DOCTRINES IN THESE PAST THREE YEARS.

MOTHER WILL BE SO PROUD OF ME.

Gandhi could hardly believe how great his mother's love for him was. She had placed him ahead of herself even at the moment of her death.

WHAT DO YOU PLAN TO DO FROM NOW ON?

I'M THINKING OF STARTING A LAW PRACTICE IN BOMBAY.

I'LL WORK FOR THE POOR AND DEFEND THE INNOCENT.

Before long, Gandhi opened an office in Bombay, a bustling capital city, and got down to business.

....

But Gandhi's office had little business, even six months after opening.

He didn't realize that people preferred English lawyers to Indian ones.

ENGLISH LAWYER

....

That was because most of the judges at that time were British. So, when Indian lawyers faced British lawyers in trials, the British lawyers usually won.

BANG

THIS IS SERIOUS DISCRIMINATION AGAINST INDIANS!

EVEN IF INDIA IS UNDER BRITISH RULE, HOW CAN THIS HAPPEN IN THE SACRED COURT...?

Gandhi was outraged at the British who broke the laws and rules, but there was practically no way to win against them.

Finally, Gandhi had to close down his office because he had no clients.

LAW OFFICE

CLOSED

Rajkot, India

Frustrated, Gandhi decided to stay in his room. He was too depressed to go out.

SIGH

It was an exciting change for Gandhi. He could practice law while living in a new environment in South Africa.

South Africa is located at the southern end of the African continent. South Africa has lots of natural minerals, including gold, copper, and diamonds.

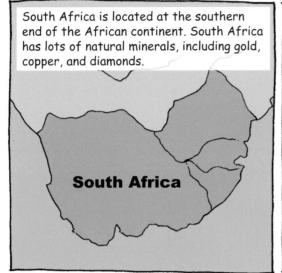

South Africa

Because of its valuable resources, South Africa was constantly being attacked by foreign armies. Like India, it was under the rule of Britain and Holland.

In May 1893, Gandhi started working at the South African branch of Dada Abdullah and Company in Durban, a harbor city in South Africa.

SOUTH AFRICA BRANCH, DADA ABDULLAH AND CO.

WELCOME!

CLAP

CLAP

His boss's concerns soon turned into reality. It happened when Gandhi left Durban for Pretoria to take care of the lawsuit.

POOR GANDHI, HE'S GOING TO LEARN THE HARD WAY...

CHUG CHUG

?

56

This incident turned Gandhi into a peace fighter
who constantly battled against British imperial rule.

EPISODE 5
NATAL INDIAN CONGRESS

THANKS FOR THE RIDE.

YOU'RE WELCOME.

SO, THIS IS PRETORIA.

Gandhi had taken three different carriages to finally reach Pretoria.

In Pretoria, the Indian people were treated much worse than they were in other regions.

Indians had to pay an outrageous amount of tax, and they could not walk in the streets after 9 o'clock at night.

I'M SURE PEOPLE WILL LISTEN TO WHAT I HAVE TO SAY HERE.

EVERYONE! WE INDIANS ARE JUST AS GOOD AS THE BRITISH ARE.

BUT WE ARE TREATED UNFAIRLY BY THE BRITISH!

While working on Dada Abdullah's lawsuit, Gandhi gave legal counsel to people who were in need of help...

...and at night he taught people English, so they could respond to the British soldiers.

As time went by, many people started to believe in what Gandhi had to say.

GANDHI IS A TERRIFIC YOUNG MAN!

TELL ME ABOUT IT. HE'S YOUNG, BUT HE'S VERY BRAVE.

I THINK WE WILL BE BETTER OFF IF WE FOLLOW MR. GANDHI!

HAHAHA

FIND PEOPLE FROM THE COMMUNITY, QUICKLY! WE WILL HAVE AN EMERGENCY MEETING!

Gandhi gathered people of his city and discussed the possible options.

This group, the "Natal Indian Congress," was formed on May 22, 1894. Gandhi became the secretary of the Congress and started the fight for the rights of Indian people. Gandhi was 25 years old.

NATAL INDIAN CONGRESS

First, Gandhi collected signatures from those who disagreed with the new law and submitted them to the British government. Over 10,000 people signed.

Then they sent letters of protest to the South African Congress and every newspaper in Britain, to let the world know about the cowardly action of the South African colonial government.

WOW, ARE THOSE ALL LETTERS?

As newspapers across Britain wrote about the racial discrimination in South Africa, British people as well as Indians started to criticize the South African colonial government.

NOW THAT IS TOO MUCH...

LONDON TIMES

LISTEN, EVERYONE'S CRITICIZING YOU. JUST CALL OFF THE NEW LAW!

MIND YOUR OWN BUSINESS!

In the end, however, the South African colonial government passed the discriminatory law. All of Gandhi's efforts were ignored.

Act to deny Indians the right to vote

Passed

I CAN'T BELIEVE WE LOST...

MAYBE OUR STRENGTH ALONE WASN'T ENOUGH.

WHAT SHOULD WE DO NOW?

I WILL PROBABLY HAVE TO RETURN TO INDIA FOR A WHILE.

INDIA HAS A GROUP LIKE OURS CALLED THE "INDIAN NATIONAL CONGRESS." I'LL ASK THEM FOR SUPPORT.

The "Indian National Congress" was a famous human rights group organized in 1885, that mainly supported education and welfare projects.

Gandhi, recognizing the limits of his power, went back to India in 1896, after three years in South Africa.

Gandhi received a warm welcome from the Indian National Congress. Gandhi had already become a famous figure in India thanks to his efforts in South Africa.

OUR BROTHERS IN SOUTH AFRICA ARE SUFFERING FROM SERIOUS DISCRIMINATION. PLEASE SUPPORT US. WE NEED YOUR HELP!

Even during his stay in India, Gandhi spoke around the country about Indian rights and wrote articles in newspapers against racial discrimination.

CLAP

CLAP

THAT BOY WENT TOO FAR···

HE'LL HAVE TO BE WARNED.

But with his increasing popularity, more people started to hate Gandhi as well···

73

The next day, the newspaper printed the story on the front page. Many people started to criticize the mobs and the colonial government.

EPISODE 6
THE FIRST VICTORY

Johannesburg, South Africa
Gandhi opened an attorney's office in Johannesburg to raise funds for his activities.

With the money he raised, he published a newspaper called "Indian Opinion" in 1904 to broadcast the problems of India to the world.

INDIAN OPINION

EXTRA! EXTRA!

EXTRA! EXTRA!

Gandhi's paper reported a terrifying story.

HUH? NO, IT CAN'T BE...

In 1906, the South African colonial government announced its plan to enact the "Asian Population Registration Act."

Asian Population Registration Act Announced

According to the act, all residents of Asian countries, including India, had to register their name, age, address, job, and other personal information with the colonial government, and carry a registration card bearing their fingerprints at all times.

If this law were passed, the government could observe Asians, including Indians, at all times and convict them at will.

VIOLENCE LEADS TO MORE VIOLENCE. IF WE ATTACK THE GOVERNMENT, THEY WILL STRIKE BACK WITH AN ARMY, AND DO MORE DAMAGE TO US.

DO NOT USE VIOLENCE EVEN IF THE BRITISH POLICE TREAT US WITH VIOLENCE.

WE WILL FIGHT AGAINST THE GOVERNMENT IN A PEACEFUL WAY.

This was the start of Gandhi's famous "nonviolence resistance movement," protesting without any violent acts.

NOW LET'S GET OUT THERE AND SHOW OUR WILL TO THE GOVERNMENT!

SATYAGRAHA! LET'S BE DEVOTED TO THE TRUTH!

DON'T LET THE PEOPLE HOLD PROTESTS!

STOP THEM!

ARE YOU STARTING A RIOT?

SEND THEM ALL HOME, UNLESS YOU WANT TO BE ARRESTED!

WE CAME OUT TO THE STREETS TO WIN BACK RIGHTS THAT BELONG TO US. HOW CAN YOU CALL THIS A RIOT?

I WILL KILL YOU, IF YOU DON'T DISMISS THE CROWD!

CLICK

NO GUN CAN THREATEN ME. THE ONLY THING I AM AFRAID OF IS A LIFE WITHOUT FREEDOM.

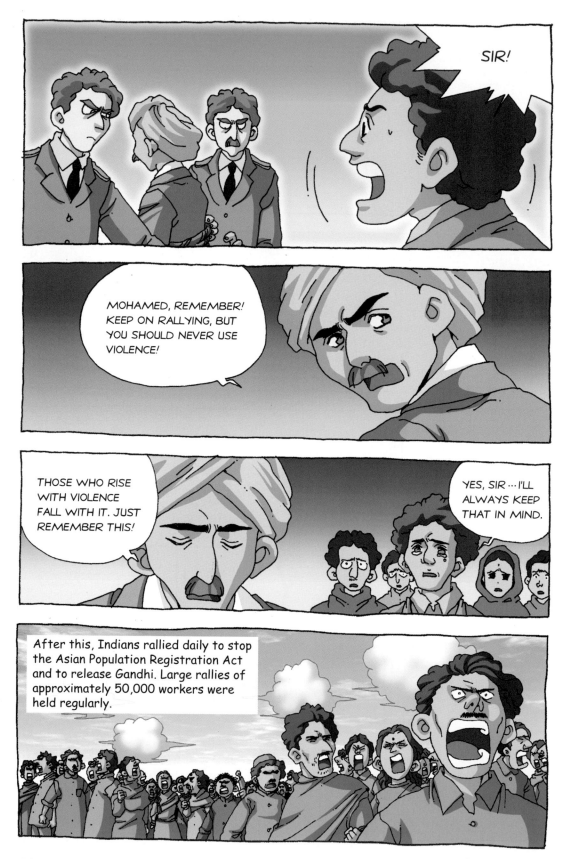

SIR!

MOHAMED, REMEMBER! KEEP ON RALLYING, BUT YOU SHOULD NEVER USE VIOLENCE!

THOSE WHO RISE WITH VIOLENCE FALL WITH IT. JUST REMEMBER THIS!

YES, SIR...I'LL ALWAYS KEEP THAT IN MIND.

After this, Indians rallied daily to stop the Asian Population Registration Act and to release Gandhi. Large rallies of approximately 50,000 workers were held regularly.

As Indians rallied without any acts of violence, the British police could not use violence against them. It all went as Gandhi had intended.

THE CROWD IS GETTING BIGGER EVERY DAY.

I THINK YOU SHOULD MEET GANDHI AND COMPROMISE.

MAYBE YOU'RE RIGHT.

LET'S GO TO GANDHI'S CELL.

After two months of rallies, the Colonial General met Gandhi in person, and suggested that he would abolish the Asian Population Registration Act, if Gandhi and his friends registered under the act.

Pleased with the offer to abolish the act, Gandhi agreed to the General's words.

OK, I'LL DO THAT.

As soon as he was released, he persuaded people to register.

THERE'S NOTHING HE CAN DO NOW THAT THE REGISTRATION IS OVER.

WE TRUSTED THE GENERAL, BUT HE BETRAYED US.

WE WILL END UP AS THEIR SLAVES, AS LONG AS WE HAVE THESE REGISTRATION CARDS.

LET'S DESTROY THIS DIRTY THING. IT MUST NOT EXIST!

FLIP

ABOLISH THE ASIAN POPULATION REGISTRATION ACT!

LET'S BURN ALL OF THEM.

In August 1908, Gandhi and 2,000 fellow Indians in Johannesburg burned their registration cards.

LET ME BURN THESE FOR YOU.

The protest continued for six years. During those six years, Gandhi and other leaders of the Natal Indian Congress were arrested and released dozens of times.

BACK AGAIN?

As the rally went national, you could hear the slogans of the movement everywhere in South Africa.

THIS COUNTRY IS BEING TORN APART!

NO RACIAL DISCRIMINATION!

ABOLISH THE ASIAN POPULATION REGISTRATION ACT!

91

I'LL HOLD A PRESS CONFERENCE. CALL THE REPORTERS.

ANNOUNCE TO ALL OF THE NATIONAL PAPERS THAT I WILL ABOLISH THE ASIAN POPULATION REGISTRATION ACT!

The Asian Population Registration Act was finally stopped in 1914, after six years of protest. All of the Indians in South Africa were hugging one another with tears of joy on that day.

After 20 years of hard work, this was Gandhi's first victory.

THIS IS ALL THANKS TO YOU, SIR!

He was then 45 years old.

THIS VICTORY IS EVERYONE'S VICTORY!

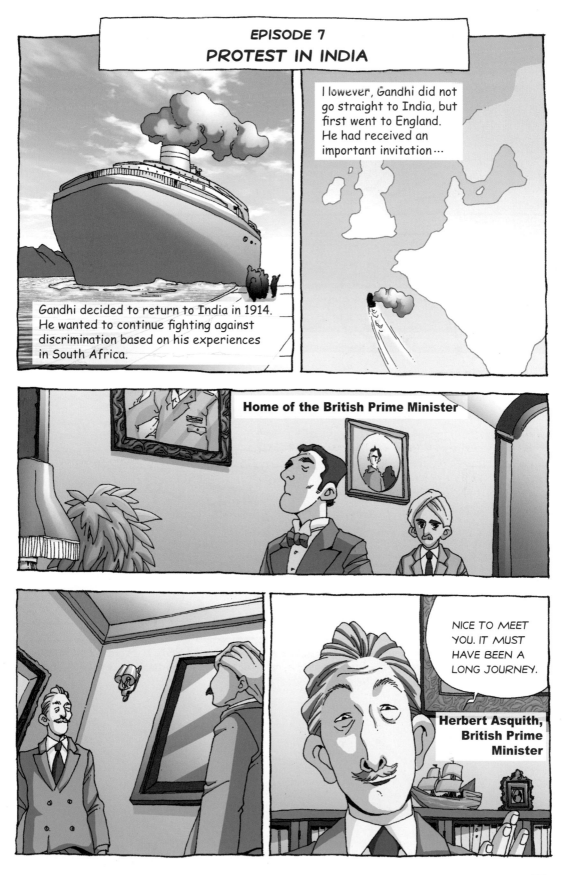

EPISODE 7
PROTEST IN INDIA

Gandhi decided to return to India in 1914. He wanted to continue fighting against discrimination based on his experiences in South Africa.

However, Gandhi did not go straight to India, but first went to England. He had received an important invitation...

Home of the British Prime Minister

NICE TO MEET YOU. IT MUST HAVE BEEN A LONG JOURNEY.

Herbert Asquith, British Prime Minister

I WONDER WHAT KIND OF BUSINESS A HIGH-PROFILE POLITICIAN LIKE YOURSELF WOULD HAVE WITH ME?

I WANTED TO SEE YOU TO DISCUSS THE WAR THAT HAS BROKEN OUT RECENTLY.

A WAR···

BUT INDIA IS NOT INVOLVED.

World War I was the global war between the Allied Powers of Britain, France, and Russia, and the Central Powers of Germany, Austria, and Turkey. The war broke out in 1914 and ended with victory for the Allied Powers.

IT'S WHAT EVERYONE IN INDIA IS HOPING FOR.

I DON'T HAVE TO HESITATE. WE SHOULD PARTICIPATE, AND WIN OUR INDEPENDENCE.

OKAY. WE WILL HELP.

I ASSURE YOU, YOU HAVE MADE A WISE CHOICE.

Gandhi made a speech in a plaza to the Indian students in England and encouraged them to participate in the war. Most people refused at first …

…but Gandhi's heartfelt persuasion led many Indian students to join the military and fight in the war.

Gandhi organized a medical and supply unit, made up of Indian people, that helped to treat the injured and supplied food and ammunition.

YOUR INJURY WILL HEAL, DON'T WORRY.

I'M ASHAMED THAT I HAVE DESPISED AND BEEN MEAN TO INDIANS IN THE PAST, AND NOW I'M GETTING HELP FROM YOUR PEOPLE.

In January of the next year, Gandhi, now healthy and fit, returned to his homeland, the country he missed so much.

GANDHI! GANDHI!

HURRAY FOR THE GREAT LEADER!

WHAT'S YOUR NEXT MISSION?

I'M GOING TO TRAVEL AROUND THE COUNTRY TO SEE HOW PEOPLE LIVE. I HAVE LIVED AWAY FOR SO LONG, I WANT TO SEE HOW INDIA HAS CHANGED.

GOOD HEAVENS!

The countryside of India was in bad shape. Farmlands had been left deserted as farmers could not afford to buy seeds for crops.

Most of the residents were very skinny because they did not have anything to eat.

IT'S TERRIBLE. HOW DID IT BECOME SO BAD?

PROBABLY BECAUSE OF THOSE HEAVY TAXES FROM THE BRITISH GOVERNMENT.

THEY IMPOSED A HUGE TAX FOR THE WARTIME FUND, AND NOW THESE PEOPLE ARE BROKE, AND CAN'T FEED THEMSELVES.

THIS IS HORRIBLE. THESE PEOPLE SHOULD HAVE THEIR FREEDOM.

BE PATIENT. THE BRITISH GOVERNMENT PROMISED TO MAKE INDIA INDEPENDENT AFTER THE WAR.

In January 1915, Gandhi gathered a group of homeless people who had no money and established the "Ashram" farm with them.

ASHRAM FARM

Gandhi and the other residents plowed, sowed, and grew crops on the farm.

Ashram prospered over time, thanks to Gandhi's outstanding leadership. The barren field became fertile soil, and their harvest grew bigger each year.

The farm solved the food problem for many poor people, and others came to see Gandhi when they heard the news. The people praised Gandhi as "the leader to save India."

Around that time, Tagore, the famous Indian poet and Nobel prize winner for literature, referred to him as "Mahatma Gandhi."

Rabindranath Tagore
(1861–1941)

MAHATMA MEANS "GREAT SOUL" IN THE INDIAN LANGUAGE.

Three years later, in 1918, Gandhi finally received the news he was waiting for.

THE ALLIES WON THE WAR?

THAT'S RIGHT. THE BRITISH GOVERNMENT JUST ANNOUNCED ITS VICTORY.

THEN THAT MEANS ...?

103

British Cabinet To Pass the Rowlatt Act

Shamelessly, the colonial government passed the Rowlatt Act, which was designed to suppress Indian people even harder. The Rowlatt Act was an outrageous law that enabled authorities "to arrest anyone who opposes Britain."

Headquarters, Indian National Congress

The Indian National Congress had an emergency meeting to discuss how they should respond to the Rowlatt Act.

DO WE HAVE TO PUT UP WITH THIS RIDICULOUS LAW?

NO, AND WE WON'T.

EPISODE 8
HARTAL MOVEMENT

On March 30, 1919, the Indian National Congress started the Hartal movement.

WHERE ARE ALL THE WORKERS?

THEY SAID THEY WON'T WORK FOR US ANYMORE.

Thousands of Indians stopped working.

CLOSED

Stores that sold imported goods from Britain closed down.

This movement soon developed into a huge resistance movement.

ABOLISH THE ROWLATT ACT!

WELL, THE GOVERNMENT CANNOT FIGHT THE PEOPLE IF WE KEEP TO THE PRINCIPLE OF NONVIOLENCE.

But not everything worked as Gandhi hoped, as some regions started to show signs of violent uprising.

On April 13, two weeks after the Hartal movement started, angry civilians clashed with the British army in Amritsar, Punjab, a city in northern India.

LET'S DRIVE THE BRITS OUT OF THIS COUNTRY!

BRITISH LIARS! GO BACK TO ENGLAND AT ONCE!

The plaza was soon filled with the wounded. On that day, 379 people were killed, and 1,000 were seriously injured by the British army.

THIS IS HORRIBLE. SHOOTING PEOPLE WITH NO WEAPONS...

PEOPLE RULED BY ANOTHER COUNTRY MUST OFTEN SUFFER TERRIBLE THINGS.

GANDHI MUST BE EVEN MORE HEARTBROKEN THAN WE ARE.

SOB SOB

In August 1920, Gandhi got even more people involved in the Hartal movement. Students refused to go to schools that had British principals...

...and people returned all medals and titles from Britain.

Even when they had legal conflicts, Indian people settled their problems through compromise, refusing to have trials in the British court.

zzzzz

But it was the boycott of British products that caused the most pain to the British government.

THE MONEY YOU SPEND ON CLOTHES FROM ENGLAND ONLY GOES INTO BRITISH POCKETS.

STARTING TODAY, LET'S THROW AWAY BRITISH CLOTHES AND MAKE OUR OWN CLOTHES.

LET'S DO IT!

WE WILL FOLLOW YOU.

INDEPENDENCE FOR INDIA!

This decision raised the boycott to a whole new level.

PLOP

Gandhi brought a spinning wheel to make thread for clothing.

A SPINNING WHEEL IS A MACHINE THAT MAKES THREAD OUT OF COTTON OR WOOL.

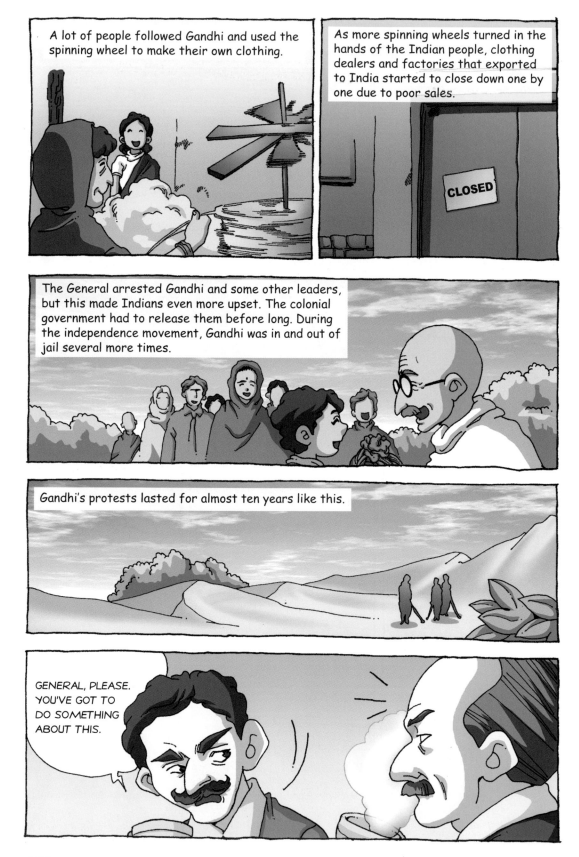

A lot of people followed Gandhi and used the spinning wheel to make their own clothing.

As more spinning wheels turned in the hands of the Indian people, clothing dealers and factories that exported to India started to close down one by one due to poor sales.

CLOSED

The General arrested Gandhi and some other leaders, but this made Indians even more upset. The colonial government had to release them before long. During the independence movement, Gandhi was in and out of jail several more times.

Gandhi's protests lasted for almost ten years like this.

GENERAL, PLEASE. YOU'VE GOT TO DO SOMETHING ABOUT THIS.

Salt Act

Indians shall not produce their own salt on, and must purchase salt made by the British government. Breaking this law will result in at least three years in jail.

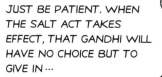

JUST BE PATIENT. WHEN THE SALT ACT TAKES EFFECT, THAT GANDHI WILL HAVE NO CHOICE BUT TO GIVE IN ...

In 1930, the British government introduced the Salt Act to discourage Indians from seeking independence.

BRITISH-OWNED SALTPAN
NO INDIANS ALLOWED

Salt contains nutrition for the human body. A lack of salt may cause death. The Salt Act tried to make Indian people give up by giving the colonial government control over the salt trade.

I NEED SALT!

BOY, IT'S HOT.

WE'LL TAKE A REST ONCE WE'RE OVER THIS HILL, SO BE STRONG FOR A LITTLE BIT LONGER.

Of course, Gandhi could not let that happen.

OKAY.

On March 12 of the same year, Gandhi traveled 320 kilometers to Dandi to make his own salt, in violation of the Salt Act. Many leaders in the Indian National Congress soon followed him.

It was a long and difficult journey for the now 61-year-old Gandhi.

Gandhi walked on bare feet under the sizzling sun. All he wore was a shabby *dhoti* cloth around his waist.

PANTING

I CAN'T KEEP UP WITH HIM ANYMORE.

H...HOW CAN HE...

WHERE DOES HE FIND ALL THAT ENERGY, AT HIS AGE?

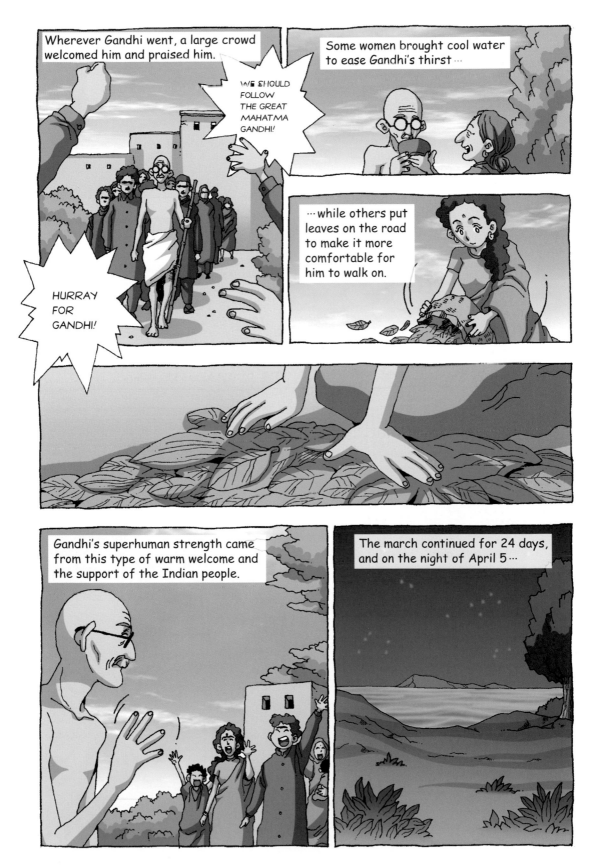

Wherever Gandhi went, a large crowd welcomed him and praised him.

WE SHOULD FOLLOW THE GREAT MAHATMA GANDHI!

HURRAY FOR GANDHI!

Some women brought cool water to ease Gandhi's thirst...

...while others put leaves on the road to make it more comfortable for him to walk on.

Gandhi's superhuman strength came from this type of warm welcome and the support of the Indian people.

The march continued for 24 days, and on the night of April 5...

...Gandhi finally made it to Dandi beach.

HURRAY!

IT'S BEEN A LONG JOURNEY, EVERYONE! LET'S START MAKING SALT TOMORROW!

At sunrise, Gandhi started to gather sea water.

The sea water soon turned into salt under the sizzling sun.

THIS IS SALT THAT GOD GAVE US. WE HAVE EVERY RIGHT TO USE THIS SALT.

I'LL EAT THIS SALT, AND SHOW THE BRITISH GOVERNMENT THAT SALT DOES NOT BELONG TO ANYONE, BUT IT IS OURS TO SHARE.

WOW!

HURRAY FOR MAHATMA GANDHI!

INDEPENDENCE FOR INDIA!

Encouraged by Gandhi's action, many Indians started to make their own salt.

But their joy did not last long.

Gandhi was arrested for this incident and put in jail for a year, until 1931.

While Gandhi was fighting against the British in India, another war broke out in Europe.

In September 1939, Adolf Hitler, the German dictator, invaded neighboring countries and started a war.

England, the U.S., and France declared war as Allied Powers against Germany. Germany struck back with its fellow Axis Powers of Japan and Italy, and it soon became a world war. This later became known as World War II (1939-1945).

WE WILL STRENGTHEN OUR RESISTANCE MOVEMENT WHILE BRITAIN IS BUSY IN A WAR AGAINST GERMANY.

THEY WILL HAVE NO CHOICE BUT TO ACCEPT OUR DEMAND FOR INDEPENDENCE.

Under Gandhi's plan, the rallies and the Hartal movement grew even stronger.

In 1942, Gandhi told Britain to "Quit India!" at a press conference with international reporters. It left the British government almost no choice.

THEY LOOK STRANGE.

NOW HE'S GETTING DOWN TO REAL BUSINESS.

HURRAY FOR GANDHI!

Indian people gathered around the jail and protested.
Angry crowds threatened the government.

FREE GANDHI!

QUIT INDIA!

INDEPENDENCE FOR INDIA!

WHAT HAPPENS IF THEY START A RIOT?

WHY WAIT TO FIND OUT? WE SHOULD SHOOT THEM ALL!

IT SOUNDS PRETTY BAD OUTSIDE. IT LOOKS LIKE THERE WILL BE A RIOT!

ONE OF US PROBABLY SHOULD GO OUT THERE AND CALM THEM DOWN.

BUT THEY WON'T LET US GO, WILL THEY?

I HAVE AN IDEA.

Gandhi started a hunger strike that day, refusing to eat food until the leaders of the Indian National Congress were released.

For the 73-year-old Gandhi, a hunger strike was very dangerous for his health.

But the warden did not know what Gandhi was capable of. Gandhi's passion for independence was far stronger than his instincts as a human being.

OK, FINE, I'LL RELEASE YOU AND YOUR FRIENDS.

WARDEN, WHAT ARE YOU DOING?

LET THEM ALL OUT!

YES, SIR!

In May 1944, the colonial government finally released Gandhi and the other independence leaders after his long hunger strike.

A year later, on August 15, World War II ended with victory for the Allied Powers.

But it was a sad victory. England had suffered serious damage from the war.

As Britain was weakening, British colonies around the globe started to demand independence for their countries.

Among those colonies, India showed the greatest desire for independence. The British could no longer ignore their demands.

One year later, March 1946

LET'S BUILD A FREE AND PEACEFUL COUNTRY! WITH THE EFFORT WE HAVE SHOWN SO FAR, INDIA CAN ONE DAY BECOME AN ADVANCED COUNTRY LIKE BRITAIN.

HURRAH

Gandhi and the National Congress helped India prepare for independent government.

But as the day of independence was drawing near, unexpected problems arose.

PEOPLE ARE TRYING TO DIVIDE THE COUNTRY?

The conflict between Hindus and Muslims was not a new issue. For a long time, they had been fighting like cats and dogs.

But when India was colonized by Britain, Hindus and Muslims had worked together to drive Britain away.

NOW IT'S MINE!

IT'S OUR COUNTRY.

NO, IT'S OUR COUNTRY.

UNITED WE STAND! LET'S DRIVE THEM OUT!

However, once Britain decided to leave, the old conflict between the two religious groups came to the surface again.

Gandhi tried everything in his power to meet with leaders from both sides and make them work together, but all his efforts were in vain.

DID YOU HEAR THE STORY?

WHAT STORY?

SIR GANDHI WENT ON A HUNGER STRIKE AGAIN.

NO WAY! HE'S FAR TOO OLD FOR THAT NOW!

On January 13, 1947, 77-year-old Gandhi started fasting again. It was his last-ditch effort to put an end to the fighting between religions.

SIR, YOU SHOULD STOP!

SHE'S RIGHT, IT COULD BE DANGEROUS. YOU ARE TOO OLD FOR THAT NOW!

On January 30, 1948, Gandhi was shot on his way to evening prayer. The man who shot Gandhi was a member of a Hindu organization that was against peace with Muslims.

Mahatma Gandhi, the great leader of India who devoted his life to his country and people, passed away.

But his spirit of love and peace shall live on forever as people remember this "Great Soul."

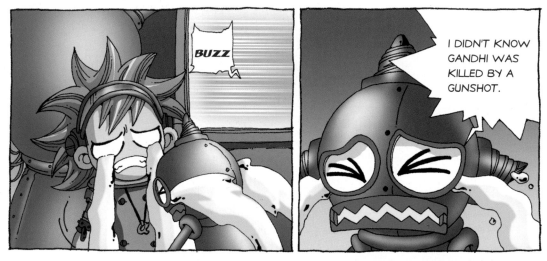

BUZZ

I DIDN'T KNOW GANDHI WAS KILLED BY A GUNSHOT.

WELL, STOP CRYING. TEARS WON'T BRING HIM BACK, WILL THEY?

BUT WE MANAGED TO CATCH GANDHI'S GREAT SPIRIT HERE.

❧ Gandhi promoted civil and economic equality, the liberation of women, universal brotherhood, an end to the caste system, and independence for India. After two centuries of British rule, India was finally granted its independence in 1947, thanks to Gandhi's nonviolent campaigns.

❧ The majority of Indians live in rural villages, and Gandhi set up organizations to defend their economic interests and develop local communities. These organizations continue to carry on Gandhi's vision today.

❧ Gandhi did not invent nonviolent resistance. He was influenced, for instance, by the example of the early American colonists boycotting British products and refusing taxes. But Gandhi was the first to understand the power of nonviolent resistance and consciously apply it to achieve change.

❧ Satyagraha—translated as "devotion to the truth," or "truth force" —is Gandhi's unique version of nonviolence, incorporating love and compassion. Gandhi knew that the power of a tyrant or unjust leader relies on the obedience of the people. His campaign used two methods: civil disobedience, meaning refusal to obey a specific law, and noncooperation, in the form of strikes, boycotts, and tax refusals. His goal was to end injustice and restore social harmony by causing a "change of heart" in his oppressors.

❧ Mohandas Gandhi was named Man of the Year by *Time* magazine in 1930, and was runner-up to Albert Einstein for *Time's* Person of the Century.

➤ Gandhi's nonviolent resistance strategy has influenced many other civil and political struggles. Martin Luther King, Jr., Nelson Mandela, and the Dalai Lama are just a few world leaders who have effectively adopted these methods. Nonviolent resistance has been used to peacefully overthrow dictators in Poland, the Philippines, South Vietnam, El Salvador, and Guatemala.

➤ In India, Gandhi is called the Father of the Nation, and his birthday is a national holiday. Indian currency bears a picture of Gandhi, as a constant reminder of how he shaped the nation. The Indian government awards the Mahatma Gandhi Peace Prize each year to people who have worked to help society.

Fun Fact

Gandhi's Watch

While Mohandas Gandhi was living and studying in England, his brother sent him a gold pocket watch. When Gandhi decided to give up his vain lifestyle and British clothes, he began wearing very simple, traditional Indian clothing, but he kept the pocket watch. He believed it was the most useful item he owned.

Gandhi carried the pocket watch throughout his entire life. He knew that there was so much work to be done that no time could be wasted. He set the clock alarm for 4 a.m. every morning, and kept all of his things very organized so he never had to waste time looking for something. Gandhi considered it rude and unacceptable to be late, and tried to make good use of every minute of his life.

When	What
1860s–70s	**1869** Gandhi is born **1874** Benjamin Disraeli is elected Prime Minister of Britain **1875** Disraeli purchases the Suez canal **1876** Britain's Queen Victoria is declared Empress of India, though she never visits the country
1880s	**1880** William Gladstone is elected Prime Minister of Britain **1882** Homes in London and New York are lit by electricity **1885** First meeting of the Indian National Congress **1887** Queen Victoria's 50-year reign is celebrated with the Golden Jubilee
1890s	**1893** Women are first allowed to vote in New Zealand **1893** Gandhi moves to South Africa, and begins to campaign for the rights of Indians **1897** J.J. Thomson discovers the electron **1897** Queen Victoria hosts the Diamond Jubilee
1900s	**1911** King George V and Queen Mary are the first British nobility to visit India **1914** World War I begins **1915** First air raid on London **1915** Machine guns and radios are installed in war planes **1917** Women begin serving in Britain's armed forces **1918** Influenza kills millions in India and Europe **1919** World War I ends

When	What
1920s	**1921** Southern Ireland gains independence from Britain **1922** Gandhi is sentenced to six years in prison for resisting British rule **1924** Novelist E.M. Forster writes *A Passage to India*, about cultural conflict in colonial India **1925** The Hindu Nationalist Party, a social organization, is formed in India **1928** British Parliament gives women equal voting rights
1930s	**1930** Gandhi's Salt March challenges the Salt Act **1932** Gandhi fasts for six days to protest the conditions of the Sudra **1939** World War II begins
1940s	**1941** Penicillin becomes widely available **1942** Gandhi launches the Quit India movement; he is imprisoned **1945** World War II ends **1947** India gains independence; Pakistan is formed **1948** India and Pakistan have their first war **1948** Gandhi is killed at age 78

On the Web

100 PICTURES OF MAHATMA GANDHI *GandhiServe Foundation*

www.photographs.gandhiserve.org/

Do you want to know what Gandhi looked like? At this site, you'll find 100 photos of Gandhi throughout his life, from childhood to his seventies. You can see Gandhi meeting with famous world leaders, playing with children, holding a hunger fast and protests, and traveling with his family.

VIDEO CLIPS OF MAHATMA GANDHI

GandhiServe Foundation

www.gandhiserve.org/footage_old.html

At this site, you can watch real video footage of Gandhi throughout his career, as he gives speeches, meets world leaders, and leads the Indian people in their fight for independence.

GANDHI STORIES *MKGandhi.org*

www.mkgandhi.org/students/introduction.htm

Here, you can find hundreds of stories and anecdotes about Gandhi as a child, student, husband, teacher, father, activist, and leader, as remembered and collected by people who knew him.

GO PLACES: INDIA *Time for Kids*

www.timeforkids.com/TFK/hh/goplaces

This website provides interactive information and activities to help you learn about different countries. Click on India to find a timeline of Indian history, a guide to India's famous landmarks, a quiz to test your knowledge of India, and an interview with an 11-year-old boy about daily life in India. You can even learn basic phrases in Hindi.

At the Library

MAHATMA GANDHI AND INDIA'S INDEPENDENCE IN WORLD HISTORY

by Ann Malaspina (Enslow Publishers, 2000)

This book traces the history of British rule in India and the leader who helped liberate his people from colonial oppression. Learn how the British first became involved in India, how Gandhi influenced British policy, and how the Indian people adapted to their newfound independence.

THE WORDS OF GANDHI

edited by Richard Attenborough (Newmarket Press, 2001)

Gandhi was a highly effective leader and a powerful speaker. This book contains hundreds of quotes by Mohandas Gandhi and excerpts from his autobiography, letters, and speeches.

I IS FOR INDIA

by Prodeepta Das (Frances Lincoln, 2004)

This A–Z book combines beautiful photographs with brief descriptions of many aspects of Indian culture. India has a rich history, complex traditions, and varied lifestyles. Learn about ceremonies, languages, wedding traditions, henna art, the national bird, and city life.

Y. kids

GREAT FIGURES IN HISTORY

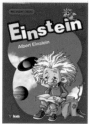

ISBN: 978-981-054942-2
May 2007

ISBN: 978-981-054945-9
June 2007

ISBN: 978-981-054946-6
July 2007

ISBN: 978-981-057555-7
February 2008

ISBN: 978-981-057552-6
February 2008

ISBN: 978-981-057551-9
February 2008

MANGA LITERARY CLASSICS

ISBN: 978-981-054942-8
May 2007

ISBN: 978-981-054943-5
June 2007

ISBN: 978-981-054941-1
July 2007

ISBN: 978-981-057554-0
January 2008

ISBN: 978-981-057553-3
January 2008

ISBN: 978-981-057556-4
January 2008

EDUCATIONAL MANGA

ISBN: 981-05-2240-1

ISBN: 981-05-2241-X

ISBN: 981-05-2766-7

ISBN: 981-05-2765-9

ISBN: 981-05-2243-6

ISBN: 981-05-2238-X

ISBN: 981-05-2239-8

ISBN: 981-05-2768-3

ISBN: 981-005-2242-8

ISBN: 981-05-2767-5